Have I ever told you?

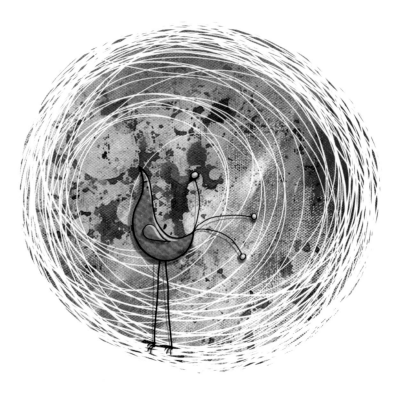

Written by Shani King

Illustrations by Anna Horváth

TILBURY HOUSE PUBLISHERS, THOMASTON, MAINE

. . . that you can be whatever you
want to be? Have I told you that you can be
a president, a doctor, a lawyer, a professor,
a firefighter, a police officer, a scientist,
an astronaut, a dancer, an inventor,
a musician, or an entrepreneur?

Have I ever told you that?

Have I ever told you...

. . . that people like you—
who look like you, who talk like you,
who speak Spanish, Arabic, English,
Swahili, Mandarin—are ambassadors,
Supreme Court justices, teachers,
chefs, artists, filmmakers, senators,
engineers, veterinarians, and writers?

Have I ever told you that?

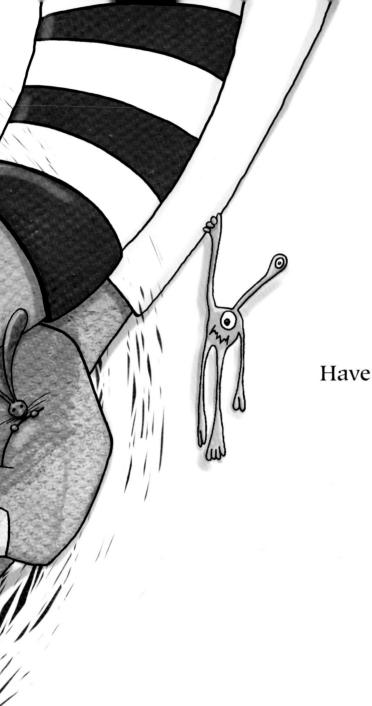

Have I told you that there is no one
more special to me than you?
That for me, you are the most
special child in the world,
and that I love you now
and will love you forever?

Have I ever told you that?

Have I told you that

you make me the happiest person in the world,

just by being you?

Have I ever told you that?

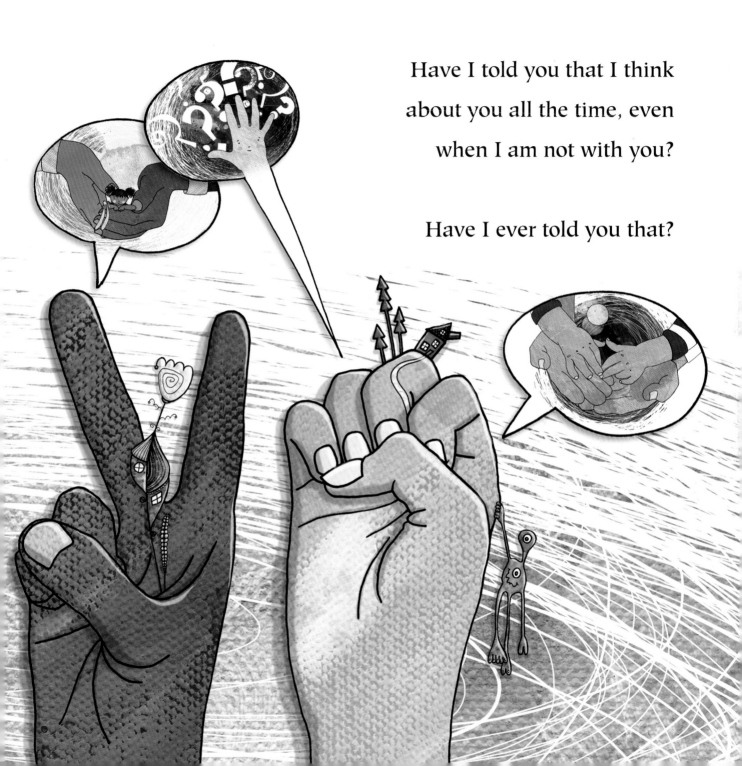

Have I told you that I think about you all the time, even when I am not with you?

Have I ever told you that?

Have I told you that you
make me laugh out loud?

Have I ever told you that?

Have I told you that I love the stories you tell and the conversations we have, and that I love to listen to you and talk with you?

Have I ever told you that?

Have I told you that
I love the way you get food
on your forehead when you eat?

Have I ever told you that?

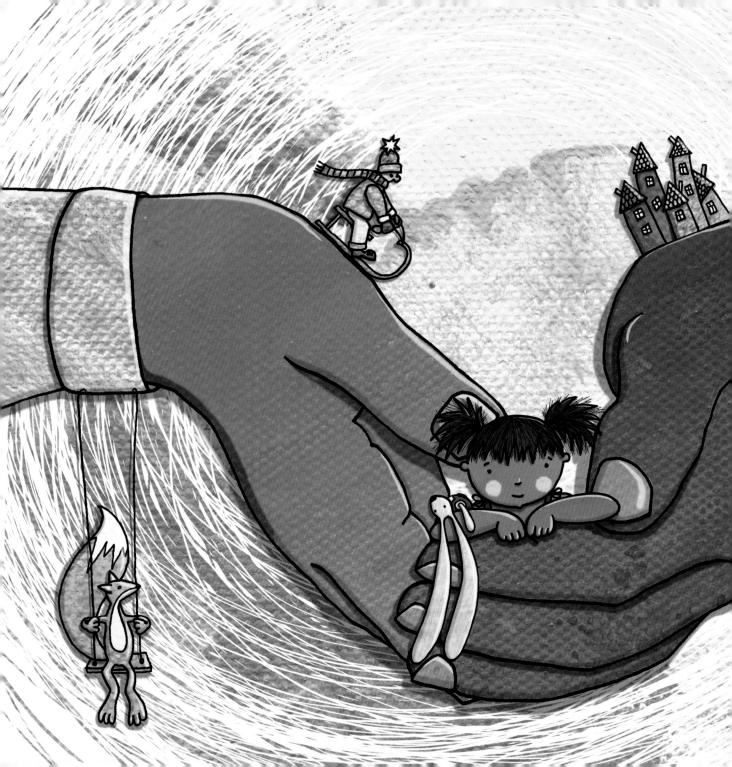

Have I told you that taking care
of you and protecting you is the
most important thing I do?

Have I ever told you that?

Have I told you that if you
hear a word that makes
you uncomfortable, you
can ask me what it means
and we can talk about it?

Have I ever told you that?

Have I told you that you should
be kind to everyone and treat
everyone with respect? That we all
deserve respect because we are all
people? And that the people you
see have friends and families who
love them just as I love you?

Have I ever told you that?

Have I told you that you should stand up for people who need help or are being picked on? People of any color, people of any faith, people of any size or shape or ability?

Have I ever told you that?

Have I told you that you should
always do the right thing, even
when the right thing is hard to do?

Have I ever told you that?

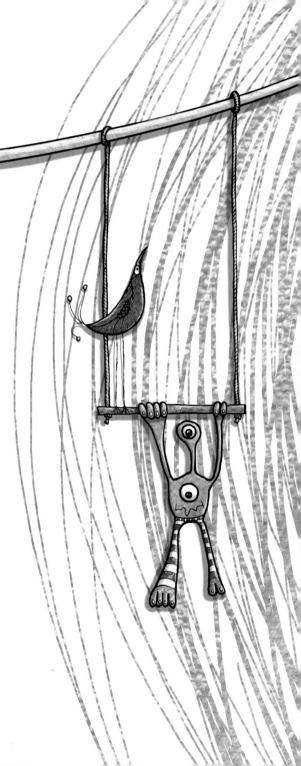

Have I told you that it's OK to disagree with someone, but you should listen to them with courtesy and respect?

Have I ever told you that?

Have I told you that you are courageous,
hardworking, smart, funny, tough,
humble, determined, patient, honest,
compassionate, kind, curious, positive,
thankful, hopeful, and wonderful?

Have I ever told you that?

Yes, I think I have.

And it is true.

I love you!

Yes, I think I have.

And it is true.

I love you!

Tilbury House Publishers
12 Starr Street
Thomaston, Maine 04861
800-582-1899 • www.tilburyhouse.com

Hardcover ISBN 978-0-88448-719-7
eBook ISBN 978-0-88448-721-0

First hardcover printing November 2018

15 16 17 18 19 20 XXX 10 9 8 7 6 5 4 3

Library of Congress Control Number: 2018953652

Designed by Anna Horvath, Annabies Art & Design, www.annabies.me
Production by Frame25 Productions

This book has benefited from the generous support of the Center on Children and
Families at the University of Florida Frederic G. Levin College of Law.
Printed in China.

SHANI KING is a professor of law and director of the Center on Children and Families
at the University of Florida. Proud father of a daughter and a son, he loves empowering
children any way he can. When not writing, he loves spending time with his wife and
children, running, reading, and playing the drums.

ANNA HORVÁTH makes colorful and magical paintings full of surprising details,
sinuous lines, and funny creatures. Her mission is to encourage children to use their
imaginations and dare to see the world differently. Anna lives in Switzerland with her
wonderful children and husband and can be visited at www.annabies.me.